REAL GHOST
SOUTHERN HAUNTINGS
STORIES

D1362180

EVE S EVANS

ALSO BY

EVE S EVANS

Fiction:
The Haunting of Hartley House
Hartley House Homecoming
The Haunting of Crow House
The Haunting of Redburn Manor

Anthologies:
True Ghost Stories of First Responders
50 Terrifying Ghost Stories
Shadow People
Chilling Ghost Stories
Haunted Hotels
Haunted Hospitals
Haunted Objects
Supernatural Creatures
Haunted Suburbs
When I Died
Paranormal 911 Calls
Haunted Hotels
True Ghost Stories: Dreadful Demonic Entities

Follow Eve and her books on Goodreads or Bookbub! And get notified of any new reads coming in 2021-2022.

The following stories are based on true events.

All rights reserved. No part of this publication may be transmitted or reproduced in any form or by any means. This includes photocopying, electronic, mechanical, or by storage system (informational or otherwise), unless given written permission by the author.
Copyright © September 2021 Eve S. Evans
Cover By: Juan Padron

For Rob

1 I HAD TO LET YOU GO

This is a story about the car that came out of nowhere and changed my life forever.

It was mid-afternoon on a weekend, and I remember the sky was particularly grey and drizzly. My son and I were in the car, talking about baseball as we drove home from the grocery store.

One minute, everything was fine. My son was smiling as he chatted away, and I was listening to him while keeping my eyes on the road. The next, something red flashed in front of us, and I slammed down on the brakes.

But I wasn't fast enough.

Everything after that happened so fast.

There was a resounding crash, and the impact threw my son and I back in our seats. Glass cascaded all around us, and I heard the sound of metal tearing and crunching. Every part of my body hurt, even as the airbag attempted to cushion the blow. All I could do was grip the steering wheel until my knuckles turned white, waiting for it all to be over.

And right beside me was my son, screaming at the top of his lungs in pure pain and terror. I don't think I'll ever forget that sound as long as I live.

At some point, the car flipped over. But I was already unconscious by then.

I woke up when the paramedics were removing me from the wreckage of our car. I couldn't move my left arm, and I was pretty positive it was broken. There was pain everywhere as the paramedics loaded me onto a stretcher. But I didn't care as I screamed for my son. I just wanted to know that my son was okay.

"Calm down, he's on his way to the hospital already," I was told by one of the paramedics.

As they folded the legs of the stretcher beneath me and lifted me into the ambulance, I saw him. The monster responsible for this. He was sitting next to his car, crying. As far as I could see, apart from a scratch on his forehead, he was uninjured.

Hot, painful tears began to stream down my cheeks, and I turned my head away, too disgusted to even look at him anymore.

The whole ride to the hospital, I only had one thing on my mind: it wasn't fair. It wasn't fair that *he* was the one who went through the red light, and he only walked away with a scratch. My son and I had done nothing to deserve this.

It was five hours before I saw my son again. It was supposed to be his birthday next week; he was supposed to be turning nine. I kept thinking what terrible timing this all was. He was supposed to be excited, getting ready for his party, trying to guess his presents. He should be living like a normal nine-year-old, not in hospital because of someone else's carelessness.

They wheeled me into his room, and my heart just sank. His head was bandaged, and he had a ventilator breathing for him. He wouldn't open his eyes or respond to me. It was like I'd already lost him.

The next day, I got the news I had been dreading. A parent's worst nightmare.

My son would never see his ninth birthday.

He was brain dead. There was no coming back from that. No chance of recovery. I had to make the call to take him off life support. The news broke me. I remember staggering around his room, too numb to walk, grasping at the bed handle to prevent my knees from buckling underneath me. I was hysterical. My son, my baby, was gone.

I'm going to skip forward to a week after the funeral. I had taken leave from work to deal with my grief. At first, I was thankful for the bereavement leave. But after a few days, I started to curse it. I thought what I needed was some time alone to process everything, but I was wrong. Being alone meant I was stuck in my head all the time. The same thoughts overwhelmed me, the same feelings of guilt and grief. In my head, all I saw was the crash, my son lying in the hospital bed on the ventilator, and the last breath he ever took.

The middle of the night, at some point during that week, was the first time something happened.

I woke up to one of my son's toys going off. It was one of his cars that made a siren noise when you pushed it. Startled and confused, I simply laid there in bed, listening with my eyes wide open until the siren eventually stopped.

After a few minutes, I finally managed to control my trembling hands and take a few deep beaths and mustered up the courage to go and investigate. I slipped out of the covers and tip-toed barefoot to his room.

Instead of going inside, I paused outside of his door and just listened, holding my breath.

Inside, it sounded like someone was playing with his cars. I could hear them clinking together as if someone was banging them into each other.

I didn't understand at first what I was hearing. Was I imagining it? But it sounded, clear as day, as though someone was inside my son's bedroom, playing with his toys.

Sucking in another deep breath, I opened the door as fast as I could and switched the light on.

There was nobody inside. But on the floor, about two feet in front of me, was a red car, a fire truck and a black car.

A few days before this, I had gone into his room and made his bed and picked up all of his toys and placed them into the bins in the closet. I was certain I hadn't missed any, and I'd shut the door after me. I couldn't bear walking past his room and seeing how empty it was.

But if I'd put his toys away – and I was certain I had gotten them all – then why were they on his floor right now? Who had put them there? Toys didn't just jump out of closets all on their own.

I held back tears as I picked the toys up and placed them back inside his closet, making sure the door was shut tight. Then I scanned the room carefully to make sure nothing else was out of place.

His clothes and shoes were all put away, and his bed was still made. Even his iPad sat untouched on the headboard shelf. I shook away my confusion, trying to convince myself that I must have simply forgotten to put them away. My head wasn't exactly at a great place, and it wasn't completely impossible I had missed them.

I gave the room one last glance, then turned the light back off and carefully shut the door behind me.

A few more weeks went by without anything unusual happening. I'd finally re-opened my son's door, and I would sometimes go inside his room and sit on his bed, talking out loud as though he was still there with me. It brought me a sense of comfort, in a way.

One night, I'd just come home from work and was putting some laundry away. The towel closet is right outside my son's room, on the other side of the hallway. As I was loading the shelves with the towels, I heard something fall to the floor behind me, coming from inside my son's room.

I shut the towel closet, turned around slowly, and walked into his room. On the floor at the side of his bed was his iPad. It had been sitting on the middle shelf of his headboard, far away from the edge. Far enough that someone would have had to smack it very hard to get it to land where it did. It definitely couldn't have fallen there on its own.

I picked it up and placed it back where it had been, cautiously inspecting the room. I was starting to feel as though I was being watched, like I wasn't alone there, and I began to consider the possibility that someone had broken into the house while I had been at work.

Trying not to appear too panicked, I went to the kitchen and grabbed a knife from the drawer, just in case. Then I went through every room, checking any hiding places and making sure all of the windows and doors were locked. There was no sign of a break-in, and no other evidence that someone could be inside the house. I was starting to think I was going crazy.

Although I tried to tell myself there were probably perfectly rational reasons for the things that had happened, I still couldn't shake away the feeling that something was definitely going on.

This was finally confirmed a few months later, when another incident occurred.

This one is what finally got me wondering if my son was still around somehow.

I had just gotten home from work again and was making dinner. I wanted something easy and quick, so I settled for mac and cheese. I set my plate on the table, at the spot I normally sat, then grabbed my cup and went to the fridge to fill it with some ice.

After I'd gotten my ice and some soda, I went back to the table to sit down.

But something made me pause. My plate was no longer sitting at my usual spot. Instead, it was further down the table, at my son's usual place.

I looked between the spot I had put the plate to where it was now in disbelief. I knew I wasn't going crazy. The plate had definitely moved.

Trying to stay calm, I moved the plate back to my spot and sat down. But I couldn't just ignore what had happened. So, after a few bits, I decided to do a test. I got up from the table, leaving my plate where it was, and went down the hallway to the bathroom. I shut the door and waited for a couple of minutes, before returning to the table.

As expected, the plate had moved again. It was now sitting right in front of the seat my son always chose.

Tears formed in my eyes again as I sat down, staring at the empty chair my plate was now sitting in front of.

I smiled, and said: "Hello, Tucker."

I sat there in silence for at least twenty minutes, unable to move or even eat any more of my dinner. I just stared at the chair and wondered if my son really was still here with me.

This is the story of the worst day of my life, and the strange incidents that followed. I still notice that things move around the house from time to time. I'm not scared of it anymore though, and I've learned to accept it as the way things are now.

I normally just shrug it off as *that's just Tucker being Tucker.*

BROTHERLY LOVE

When my brother was eighteen, he died in a car accident. I was sixteen at the time, and I was devastated.

Over the course of the last two years in my parents' home, I have had several experienced where I felt as though he was trying to communicate with me.

The first time it happened was in the middle of the night. I'd woken up from a nightmare and decided to go downstairs to get a glass of water and calm myself down.

At the time, my brother's ashes were sitting on the fireplace mantle in the living room, which was located to the right of the kitchen. The door between the two rooms was usually open, so you could see into the living room quite clearly on the way to the kitchen.

I had not turned any lights on in the house as I was trying not to wake my parents, whose bedroom was also downstairs.

So, I was half-way to the kitchen, walking through the near-complete darkness, when out of the corner of my eye, I saw the black silhouette of a person standing in the living room, right by the fireplace where my brother's urn was.

I was still a little spooked from the nightmare I'd just had, so I hurried to the kitchen and flipped on the light switch as quickly as I could. When I turned back and looked through the door to the fireplace, the silhouette was gone. Even though it was dark, I was sure there had been someone standing there.

I found myself wondering if it had been my brother. They had been standing directly beside the urn that held his ashes, and as the days passed and I went over the moment in my head, I realized that the shadow had been the same height and build that my brother had been. I convinced myself it had been him.

On another occasion, after basketball practice, I had climbed into my car and leaned over the seat to put my backpack onto the backseat, when I was suddenly overwhelmed with the smell of my brother's cologne. It so sudden and so strong, as though he had been sat right there.

The next morning, when I got into my car, I expected the smell to still be lingering, but it had already disappeared.

A few weeks later, something else happened. I have this bad habit of leaving the fridge door open, which used to drive my brother insane. He'd always walk in and shut the door and give me a lecture about it. But it was a habit I could never seem to shake.

It was the weekend, and my parents had gone for a bike ride at a park close to our house, so I was alone.

Around lunchtime, I got hungry and went downstairs to make myself a sandwich. As usual, I forgot to shut the fridge door, and left it open for about ten minutes.

I remained in the kitchen this whole time, looking out the window as I ate my sandwich. I remember that our creepy neighbor was arguing with the mailman again.

As I watched them, I heard a whoosh behind me, and then the sound of the fridge door being shut. By the time I turned around and looked, there was nothing there – but the fridge was definitely shut. There was no way it could have closed on its own. No windows were open, and there was no breeze. Plus, the fridge door itself was too heavy for anything other than a person to shut it. But I was alone.

After the fridge incident, nothing else happened for over half a year.

I used to take forever getting ready in the bathroom on a morning, which was another thing that used to irk my brother to no end. He actually ended up developing his own knock which basically translated to: "Get out of the bathroom, now."

It was the morning of our school picture day, and I was taking a longer time than usual getting ready and making sure my hair was perfect. I was curling my hair and was almost done when I heard it. Someone knocked on the bathroom door. And it was my brother's knock.

I almost burnt myself on the curling wand when I jumped at it. I turned around, and just stared at the door for the next few minutes, not sure what to do. Part of me was almost scared to open the door. Nobody else knew about that knock except for me and my brother; not even my parents would know it. And yet I was certain it was the same.

Finally, I set down the curling iron, took a deep breath, and reached for the door. I opened it in one short, sharp movement, not wanting to delay any longer, and looked out. The hallway was empty. I peeked my head out further and looked left, then right. But there was nobody out there.

I never could debunk or explain any of these events. They were too specific to my brother's behavior. I think it really was him, letting my know that he was still there, watching over me.

When I turned eighteen, I moved out of my parents' house and now live in an apartment with my best friend. Since the move, nothing unusual has ever happened, and I still leave the fridge door open for long periods of time…

PAWS IN THE SNOW

My beloved little Pomeranian passed away when she was twelve years old, after a hard year of battling cancer.

I had taken her to see the vet several times in that last month due to her worsening condition, but the vet could do nothing but give her medication for the pain. It hurt to see her suffering like she was, and so I had eventually broken down and scheduled her to be euthanized. Two days before her appointment, she passed away in her sleep. I was told by the vet that it had been a very peaceful way to go. Part of me was glad she had passed at home, where she was the most comfortable.

I brought Sammy to the vet shortly after to get her cremated; the vet took imprints of her paws and placed them on top of the box I placed her ashes in.

For the first few weeks, I was pretty depressed. Nothing was the same without her. I know it might sound silly, but I ended up placing her urn box on my nightstand, so that she could still sleep next to me, even after she had passed on. At night, I would talk to her and tell her about my day, and how much I missed her in my life. I'd recount if I had seen any squirrels running amuck in the complex, or if Mrs. Deitz's spaniel was causing a racket again. Those were her favorite things that used to excite her.

Mrs. Deitz and her spaniel lived in the apartment next to mine. He would whine the whole day if she was out running errands, and it would drive Sammy nuts. When I took Sammy outside to do her business, if she saw a squirrel, she would get this serious look on her face and stand up on her hind legs, sniffing the air as she watched the furry creature scamper across the grass. She was absolutely enthralled by squirrels. She never barked at them or chased them, merely observed them on her hind legs.

I would take Sammy everywhere with me, even when I went on holiday. Her favorite trip that I ever took her own was when we went to Hawaii. So, when my mom and I planned a trip to Hawaii a few months later, I brought her ashes with me.

After spreading her ashes, I returned home. And that's when a few unusual things happened.

Around this time, the seasons had begun to change, and it had started to snow. We got about four inches during that first snowfall.

I lived in an apartment complex that was only two floors high; I lived upstairs on the right, with Mrs. Deitz living on the left of the stairs.

The morning after it had snowed, I remember looking out of my kitchen window at the playground, admiring the large snowflakes as they cascaded down to the lawn below. I was not one who normally loved cold weather, but the first snowfall was beautiful.

As I was leaving for work, I approached the stairway after locking my door, and happened to look down. That's when I noticed the paw prints in the freshly fallen snow. I spun round, trying to follow where the prints led. They went right up to my door, and then stopped. I was stumped. There were no retreating paw prints returning down the stairs or going anywhere else. There was only a single set of prints that led to my door, and then just stopped. As though whoever had made them had simply… vanished.

At first, I wondered if the prints might have been from Mrs. Deitz's spaniel, but that was impossible. Her spaniel was three times the size of Sammy, and there was no reason her prints would have simply stopped at my door. And, after having her paw prints put on her urn box, and looking at them every night before bed, there was only one answer – those were Sammy's prints. They were unmistakable, as impossible as it sounded. But I knew they belonged to my Sammy.

I thought about that incident for the next few weeks and mentioned it to anyone who would listen. I was mesmerized by the whole ordeal. I never once thought I had imagined it or was going mad; those prints had been clear as day, and there was no other explanation. It made me wonder if that meant my Sammy was still here with me, even after death.

I got my answer not long afterwards.

When she was alive, Sammy had this one habit with her food bowl that used to drive me nuts. She used to nudge her bowl all around the kitchen, almost as though she was playing with it instead of her toys. I was constantly moving the bowl back and tripping over it when she moved it again.

After she'd passed, I didn't have the heart to pack away her things just yet. I left her toys out, and her food bowl was exactly where it had been the day she'd died, on the floor to the left of the refrigerator.

One evening, after work, I was making myself dinner. I was certain the food bowl was in its normal spot, as I saw it when I went to get something from the fridge. Later that evening, when I returned to the kitchen to wash my dishes, her food bowl had moved. It was now next to the garbage can on the other side of the room.

I knew it had moved. I was certain it hadn't been there before, and there was nothing in the kitchen that could have moved it all the way to the other side of the room. Sammy had done it.

This still happens to this day. Some days it doesn't move at all, and on others it only moves a little, as though something nudged it away. Then there are some days where I can tell she's really trying to get my attention, and she'll move it really far away from its usual spot.

I always pick the bowl up and move it back to the place by the fridge. That way, I still know that she's still with me.

I've never seen anymore paw prints in the snow, like I had that first winter. So that's a memory I will cherish forever. It was her spirit coming home.

Some people say that animals can't have souls. But in my experience, I am certain they do.

SCENTED

In 2007, I lost my grandmother. She was seventy-six years old when she came down with pneumonia and spent over a month in hospital trying to fight it. The doctors gave her three rounds of antibiotics to try and combat the infection, but nothing worked. The treatment hardly even phased it. After all, three rounds failed, my grandma decided to stop any further medical treatment. The doctors suggested other treatments, but nothing was guaranteed to work, and my grandma was tired of fighting. In the end, she asked us all to let her go.

I was heartbroken. I was really close with her growing up and shared a lot of fond memories. She was the one who had taught me how to bake and crochet, and I spent a lot of summers at her house while my parents were at work. I wasn't ready to lose her.

At first, I tried to fight the idea, and persuade her to keep trying. But in the end, I forced myself to relive the last month of her suffering to understand her decision. The illness had made her weak and bed bound. It wasn't much of a life for her, and she wanted to let go. I understand that now, but at the time it was difficult to accept.

On the week of Mother's Day, I went and visited her. The doctors had put her on morphine to ease the pain, so she was quite out of it. I brought her some flowers and a card, but when I walked into her room, she barely even seemed to recognise me. It broke my heart seeing her with such a blank, searching look on her face. It was almost like I was already losing her, and she hadn't even left yet. She wasn't the same as the woman I had once known.

She asked me who I was, and what I wanted. The whole time, I was trying to hold back my tears as I patiently explained why I was there. She seemed to accept what I was saying, but there was still no familiarity, no clear recognition of me.

After the visit, I went straight home and took a shower. I had a date in a few hours, and while I didn't feel much like going, I figured it might help distract me from my feelings.

While I was showering, I began to smell something. At first it was faint, but it began to grow stronger, until I recognised it: it smelled like flowers and sunshine, like a meadow in summer. I ignored it until I finished my shower, thinking nothing of it. Maybe it was the scent of my shower gel, or something from outside.

But when I wrapped the towel around me and stepped out of the shower, the smell was everywhere. My whole bathroom was filled with this scent. It was almost overpowering. Part of me recognised the smell from somewhere, but I couldn't quite put my finger on it.

I dried my hair and got dressed, the smell still lingering around me. Then I reached for my cell phone and noticed that I'd received multiple texts and missed calls from my mom. What I read broke my heart. My grandmother had finally passed away, just five minutes ago from the time I was reading.

Then it clicked. That smell – it was exactly what my grandma smelled like. It was her scent, the one I had grown up with.

I ran back to the bathroom, hoping that the smell would still be lingering, but it was gone. There wasn't even a trace of it left behind.

I truly believe that it was her. She was saying goodbye to me before she left.

FADED SMOKE

Growing up, my mom and I were really close. We did almost everything together. Whether it was cooking a family meal, shopping for clothes or watching television, we did it all side by side. She was more than just my mom, but my best friend, the only person in the world I felt like I could talk to.

When she was fifty-four, my mom died from a massive heart attack. It was unexpected. There had been no warning signs, nothing to prepare me. It just happened, and it turned my life upside down. I went from having my mom as my best friend, to having nobody.

I'd never felt so alone. I became self-destructive while dealing with the loss. It hit me really hard, and I thought I'd never recover from it. I'm not going to lie; it was a terribly tough time for me. It got to the stage where I would run red lights, hoping to get hit by another car, or walk across the street when the crosswalk was still red. I was eating poorly, barely sleeping.

In that month after her death, I was a complete mess. I didn't think I'd get through it.

But then it happened. One night, after spending almost an hour crying in the shower, I toweled off, got dressed and laid down on my bed. I felt exhausted, in a way that was beyond sleep. So instead, I reached for the remote, intending to watch some television until I eventually dozed off.

Before I could even turn the television on, a strange white light pierced through my curtains.

At first, I thought it might be headlights from a passing car. But I lived on the second floor of the apartment building, and it wouldn't have been so bright.

Curious, I stood up and went over to the curtains, intending to see what could be causing such a bright light. It was almost like someone was shining a torch directly into my window.

I parted the curtains and looked out. The sky was dark, and the moon was full and high. But what caught my attention was the bright, smoky mass that seemed to hover right next to the moon. It was shining directly towards my window.

I had no idea what it was. The edge of the mass was moving, almost like it was made up of static. It's so hard to describe, it was unlike anything I had seen before.

Then, just as sudden as it had appeared, it faded into nothing.

I wondered if I had imagined it, but I knew I hadn't. Whatever it was, it had been real. A light brighter than anything I had ever seen.

I stood at the window, staring up at the moon for another five minutes, hoping it would return. But it didn't. I never saw anything like that again.

I truly think that the light was from my mom. It was a message, telling me that it was okay to let her go, that I should stop trying to end my life because I didn't know how to live without her. It was her telling me I would never be alone, because she was still out there, watching over me.

WEATHER  MAN

I was barely out of high school when my father passed away. I had just celebrated my eighteenth birthday the month before, and the news was devastating.

My father and I had always been exceptionally close. He loved fishing, and out of us three girls, I was the only one who loved it as much as he did. I always enjoyed spending time with him, especially outdoors. Every time he packed up his tackle box, he would come and ask me if I wanted to go. He'd barely finish speaking before I would run and grab my fishing shoes and my favorite pole, and we were off for the day with our packed lunches and a flask.

Three days after his death, I was sleeping when I woke up suddenly to the feeling of something sitting at the foot of my bed.

Groggy and half-asleep, I sat up, rubbed my eyes, and squinted through the darkness. At the foot of my bed was a silhouette, watching me.

Somehow, I knew it was my dad. Even though his features were faded, and he was little more than a shadow than a fully formed person, I knew it was him.

"Dad?" I whispered, my voice sounding loud in the silence.

In my head, I thought I saw him smile. "Have the funeral on Friday," he said. "It will stop raining on Friday." That was all he said, before he disappeared.

I was confused, and a little startled. Why, out of everything he could have said, did he care what day we had his funeral? I didn't, at any point, doubt that I had seen him sitting at the end of my bed. Even though I was half-asleep, it had felt so real.

The next morning, I went downstairs to find my mom sitting at the table throwing a fit.

I sat down next to her, placed my hand on hers and assured her that everything was going to be okay. I reminded her that she wasn't alone; we were all there for her and would get through it together.

After guiding her through a few deep breaths, she began to calm down, and told me what was wrong. She was fretting over which day to schedule the funeral because the forecast looked terrible all week, and she didn't want everyone getting all wet and muddy if the weather was bad.

I rolled my eyes, and said to her: "Mom, do it on Friday."

She looked at me. "But it might rain on Friday."

"Trust me, do it on Friday."

She searched my face and, seeing that I was sincere, finally nodded. I sat there while she made the call to schedule the funeral for Friday.

I smiled slightly to myself, finally understanding what my father had meant when he came to me. He must have known that the funeral planning was stressing my mom out and wanted to help her out.

We had the funeral on Friday, and to my mom's pleasure, the weather cleared. The day was bright and sunny, without a single droplet of rain.

REPLICA

This story begins a few years ago, during the time my boyfriend Anthony's mom passed away.

At the time, we had been dating no longer than about six months. Both of us were in our senior year of high school, and still naïve to some degree.

His mother was only forty-five when she passed away. It was the worst thing I could imagine having to go through at our age. My heart truly felt for him and the harsh and sudden loss that happened right at the start of his journey into adulthood.

They had known she didn't have long since she was diagnosed a year before. She'd attended a doctor's check-up after she started to feel off; it was like her body was struggling to keep up with everything. Some days she would get really exhausted, and she would often experience waves of nausea and dizziness. At first, she assumed she'd contracted two different strains of flu, which had just knocked her body down for the whole month. But after Anthony and his father nagged at her to run some tests, the results were like a slap in the face. She was more ill than any of them had thought.

Anthony told me that she'd seemed completely happy and healthy in the months and years before; nobody had seen it coming at all.

In her final week, she was placed into a nursing facility with around-the-clock hospice care. It was obvious that her time was nearly up. She'd been having a lot of bad days, and it had gotten to the stage where it seemed that the good ones were a thing of the past.

I had gone with Anthony to the nursing home to see her during that last day. It broke my heart to see his mother look so ill. Her voice was terribly hoarse, and she could hardly get any words out to her son. He offered to get her a glass of water, but I insisted I'd get it so that he could have a longer visit with his mom.

With a nod from Anthony, I slipped out of her room and into the hallway. As I walked to the nurse's station, I was scrolling through the missed texts on my cell phone and didn't notice there was someone walking towards me.

I almost bumped into a woman as she was going past. When I went to apologize, something made me stop. The woman, I noticed, was wearing the same clothes as Anthony's mother. I figured it could have been a coincidence, but as she passed by, I caught a glimpse of her face. It was Anthony's mother, there was no doubt. The woman had the exact replica of her features. She smiled at me as she passed, and I followed her over my shoulder as she walked down the hallway. As I fully turned around to face her, she disappeared. Like she had never been there to start with.

It took everything I had not to think I had gone insane. Had I just imagined everything, or had Anthony's mother really just walked by me? But she should have been in her bed, too weak to even get up.

I quickly fetched the water from the nurse's station, carrying it back to the room. Sure enough, Anthony's mother was still in bed.

I tried to shake off what I'd seen, still not sure if my eyes had deceived me, or if my mind had fabricated the entire thing.

As I set the glass of water on the table next to his mother, Anthony turned to me. "I think she fell asleep."

When I looked at her face, she seemed to be smiling faintly, as though she was at peace. Maybe knowing her son was here had put her at ease. As quietly as I could, I sat down in the chair a few feet away from him and his mother.

Almost as soon as I sat down, the machines that Anthony's mom was hooked up to suddenly came to life with a cacophony of alarms and high-pitched beeps.

Nurses and doctors ran into the room, and Anthony and I watched as they went to the screens, monitoring the flat line displayed on one of them. Her heartbeat had stopped.

They ushered us out into the hallway as they began performing CPR.

Anthony was sobbing, and I was trying to console him, but I was still thinking about the woman I had seen in the hall. What if it really had been Anthony's mom?

They tried for ten minutes to bring her back to life, but she was already gone.

To this day, I cannot forget what I had seen. Anthony's mom had been walking down the hallway at the same time she should have been in her hospital room, before disappearing completely. I know it doesn't make sense, and at the time we were going through a lot; it made more sense that I had simply imagined it.

I never told Anthony about it. We've been married for two years now, with our first daughter on the way. I always felt that telling him the truth might hurt him more than it would help him. I don't want to bring up memories from such a low point in his life.

One day, I will tell him though. And I hope he forgives me for waiting so long.

MESSAGES

My mother passed away right at the end of summer. She had been diagnosed with cancer about a year before, so her passing didn't come as a complete shock, but it was still devastating to us all.

One day, while I was still grieving, I went down to the basement to watch some of our old VHS tapes on the VCR that I kept down there. I wanted to relive some of the memories I had with my mother, to ease the longing I was feeling to see her again.

I picked a tape from one of my kids' birthdays and slid it into the tape rewinder to make sure it would start from the beginning. At first, it seemed as though the rewinder was working, but then it clicked off, as though the tape was fully rewound already.

I simply assumed that whoever had watched it last time had rewound it themselves before putting it away. Thinking nothing of it, I placed it into the VCR and hit play.

To my dismay, it began playing from the middle of the tape. My mom was smiling and waving at the camera, saying "I love you!" as she blew a kiss.

With a frown, I ejected the tape and put it back in the rewinder. After only a few seconds, it clicked again. I knew there was no way it had rewound the tape in such a short amount of time, so I put it back into the VCR and attempted to manually rewind it from there. Even the VCR stopped only a short while after, acting as though the tape had been fully rewound.

Defeated, I hit play and sat back. As I expected, it started playing from the same spot as before, with my mom waving and smiling at the camera. Her voice was slightly crackly as she said: "I love you".

Instead of letting it play, I ejected the tape in frustration and turned it over in my hands a few times, inspecting it for damage. But there was nothing, no scratches or blemishes. I didn't understand why it wasn't rewinding properly. I eventually discarded the tape back into the box and picked out another, hoping I'd have better luck with a different video.

I went through the same process as before, slotting the tape into the rewind machine and waiting for it to go back to the beginning, then putting it in the VCR and hitting play.

This tape was from Christmas Eve thirteen years ago, when we'd thrown a party with the entire family. From when the tape started up, it showed my mom again, chuckling as she bounced one of my daughters on her knees.

Her eyes lit up with laughter as she bounced her slower and then faster, and my daughter giggled with those mischievous little laughs she used to do. But then, almost as though the tape had a mind of its own, my mom turned to face the screen, and I felt like she was intentionally staring right at me as she said, "And don't you forget it."

The tape went blank all of a sudden, then the screen was filled with snow as the next clip played. I hit eject on the tape and sat there, dumbfounded. Something was going on here. Although I didn't want to believe it, I couldn't help but think my mom was trying to communicate with me through these tapes.

After putting the tape away, I decided to wait for a few hours, until the kids got home from school and had dinner, before trying my luck again. I needed to know if the rewinder really was broken or if, in that moment in time, something paranormal really had happened.

The kids got home from school and did their homework while I finished up dinner, but I couldn't get my mind off the tapes.

I love you… and don't you forget it.

Was it really my mom trying to talk to me?

After we ate, I asked my oldest daughter, Jennie – who was seventeen at the time – to go downstairs and help me with something. She was glad to help and didn't ask too many questions.

I was slightly apprehensive about trying it again, but when we got downstairs, I motioned for Jennie to sit next to me in front of the television, and I explained to her what had happened earlier that day.

She seemed curious more than anything, and I was glad she didn't immediately think I was losing it.

"So, you think grandma is sending you messages?"

When she put it into words, I realized how silly it sounded. But it was the only explanation I could come up with for why the tapes wouldn't rewind, and why they seemed stuck on these specific parts, where my mom was speaking directly to the camera.

"I don't know," I admitted. "I could just be losing my mind, who knows? But either these two tapes are simply broken and won't rewind, or there is something going on here that I can't explain."

I picked the birthday tape back out of the box and placed it back into the rewinder. As before, it clicked almost immediately, without actually trying to rewind it. Slightly annoyed, I popped it into the VCR and sat back to let it play with my daughter beside me.

This time, the tape started up a few seconds earlier than the last time I had watched it.

"Well, don't you look beautiful today, little miss…"

My mom's voice trailed off as she held my daughter (Jennie) up in the air and twirled her around in circles. Jennie smiled fondly beside me as the younger Jennie on the screen laughed and kicked out her legs.

Then came the part where she repeated, "I love you", staring directly at the camera.

Jennie looked at me, and I looked back at her, searching her face for any kind of emotion.

"Was that weird?"

"I'm not sure," she said, glancing back at the television screen, which was paused on my mom's face. "It didn't sound like she was necessarily talking directly to me right now. It could have just been the spot that the tape was left off on."

I understood what she was saying, but I was unwilling to accept it was something as simple as that.

I pulled the tape out of the VCR and put an entirely different one in that I hadn't yet watched. If this did the same, then something was definitely happening.

I motioned for Jennie to push the play button, and we sat back.

The tape began with static. Then, as the video began to play, these weird horizontal lines appeared over the top. It was beginning to seem like this tape was a complete dud. The lines blocked the picture beneath, and it was almost impossible to make out what was happening in the video at all.

Jennie reached for the eject button, but I quickly slapped her hand away. "Wait," I hissed at her, leaning closer to the television. "Listen!"

Amongst the faint waves of static, we could both hear the words: "Forever… in… my…heart."

Then the sound cut off, and there was nothing but the static lines and messed-up picture.

"No way," Jennie said as she hit the rewind button, playing the video from the start again. We watched as the tape started with static, before moving to the illegible video.

But those four words – spoken in my mother's voice – never sounded again during the entire tape. We watched it for a good ten minutes, not even focusing on the video itself but for any words, but there was nothing. No audible sounds at all.

"Do you believe me now?" I asked her, climbing to my feet after shutting off the television and tucking the tapes back into the box.

Jennie nodded slowly, almost in a daze. "Yes, I do," she said. "I heard grandma. That was her voice, wasn't it?"

"Yeah, I think it was."

That was the only paranormal thing that has ever happened to me in my life, or in my house. I might not have believed it really was my mom trying to communicate with me through the tapes if my daughter hadn't heard them too.

SUDDEN

Bean was my golden lab. She was nearing ten years old, and a sudden illness struck her and would not leave. She was constantly coughing, out of breath, walking much slower, you name it.

As hard as it was for me, I knew her time was nearing. Sometimes, I would hear her coughing after I went to bed, and I would lay down beside her dog bed and just rub her back. She deserved so much love, that dog was my world.

I finally relented and had her put down. My heart was broken into a thousand pieces. Each one a shattered memory from our lives together.

I did have another dog actually, her brother Sven. I'd watch Sven search the house for her in the few weeks after her passing and it just broke my heart.

One evening before bed, I was in the living room starting to turn off lights and fold up blankets so I could go to sleep. Out of the corner of my eye, I saw the shadow of a dog walk into my bedroom.

I called over my shoulder while folding my favorite quilt, "Sven not yet! You haven't gone potty yet."

A few seconds later, not enough time for Sven to hustle out of the bedroom, I felt his nose against my bare leg. I looked down and he was sitting upright, his tail wagging on his bed. He'd never left his dog bed at all.

A little creeped out, I went back to the bedroom and investigated. I turned the light on and rummaged around to find nothing amiss.

I had to wonder, was that Bean? Was she still here? I couldn't get the thought out of my mind that night.

After a few days, I had forgotten about the ordeal. I was lying in bed watching some television and had let Sven up on the bed to cuddle with me.

Suddenly, we both heard what sounded like a possible prowler in the house. Sven was lowly growling, and I was shaking.

I finally mustered up the courage to investigate. Once out in the living room, I flipped the switch on and gasped. I have a bin for all the dog toys, and it was laying on its side, its contents spilled all over the floor. All of the toys were put away before we'd gone to bed that night.

To top it all off, Sven was sitting at my feet, staring off into space at the wall. I watched him closely, trying to decide if I needed to be freaked out. He let out this low whine and started wagging his tail. For a few minutes I just watched him, then the wall. I observed him until his tail finally stopped wagging and he turned his face up to me as if to say, "It's gone now, mom."

I picked up all of the toys, placed them back in the toy bin, sat it upright and walked around the house checking doors, windows and closets for some peace of mind. Nothing was out of the ordinary. No one was in the house.

Finally, this brings me to the last unexplained event. This one had to be about a month after Bean was gone.

I'd felt cooped up with my grief in the house, so I'd taken Sven to the lake to have some fun. I'd packed a lunch for myself and brought a ball and some towels.

Sven loved playing fetch in the water. Him and Bean could do it for hours in the summer. I was excited to get some time to play with him.

Sven was having a blast jumping in and retrieving. After a while, he finally got worn out.   Panting heavily, he sat to my right refusing to budge when I'd bring my arm up to fake throw the ball.

That's when I heard it. The whine. It only lasted a split second but there was no denying it. It sounded like my Bean!

Bean had a unique whine. She also loved fetch. I knew it wasn't Sven for two reasons. First, Sven's whine is deeper and second, Sven's ears perked up at the sound and his panting mouth slowly closed, showing his concentration on the noise.

Sven and I sat there in silence after that for a moment. I wondered if he was thinking what I was thinking and eyed him as the time passed by.

That was the only whine we'd heard like that. I'm pretty sure after these experiences that my Bean stayed with us, at least for a little while. And I'm glad because I needed her to be there while I healed.

BEST FRIENDS FOREVER

My best friend of forty years phoned me one afternoon with some completely devastating news. She had been diagnosed with cancer and not given much time.

Over the years, we'd both migrated around and did not live extremely close anymore. So, we decided to make the best of the next few months and do our best at visiting each other more.

Obviously, not long after her diagnosis, her health began declining significantly and I had to be the one to travel to her more often.

She made it five months. Five short months I'd had my best friend the center of my life again before she was off to her ever after.

I was very sad. Somedays I'd be in my pj's for longer than I should. Other days, I'd glance out the window at the sunshine and know that I should be enjoying the warmth on my skin, but I just wasn't ready to set aside my heartache and venture out just yet.

It had only been a few days after her passing and I would talk out loud to her, hoping she might be able to hear me. I was sitting in bed just before turning my light out, apologizing that I'd been so busy over the years and had not seen her more before the end. I'd turned out my bedside light and laid my head on the pillow.

Just as I was drifting off, the theme song from Toy Story, You've Got a Friend in Me sounded on the stereo downstairs.

I was shocked to say the least. I went downstairs to shut it off, only to find that, by the time I got to the stereo, it was already off again. It was mind-boggling.

Another time my husband and I were having dinner. I had hung a picture of my best friend and myself on one of the walls in our dining room. It was from a time in our teens when we had gone to a theme park together and had a blast.

We had just sat down to eat, and we were talking about my friend, her life, how much I missed her and how I hoped her husband was coping okay.

The picture frame scraped a little bit against the wall like it was being slightly tugged, then crashed to the floor.

We both watched the broken mess with wide eyes. It was freaky. I wish I could explain it away as a loose nail or something, but we'd just hung it. And it had juggled a tad before it fell, scraping against the wall. It really sounded like someone had tugged it until it fell and crashed to the floor.

We were both a little on edge after that. In fact, my husband would avoid conversations about my friend entirely after that.

For example, I'd go in the bathroom to brush my teeth and start talking to him about her while he was in the bedroom. When I'd received no response, I'd rinse my mouth, walk into the bedroom and see he'd walked out of the room entirely. I didn't blame him. It was freaky. I guess he just didn't know how to process what had happened.

We were so close that, back in elementary school, we had referred to ourselves as "the 2." It was just a nickname we made up thinking it was a cool code name. We'd hang out in a fort we made in her backyard. She lived on three acres, half of which was trees and pretty dense foliage.

We'd found the perfect spot to dodge into and make a fort. At one point, we'd even made our own flag to hang outside on some of the brush with the number two on it.

So, this happened nearly a year after my friend's passing. I was taking a shower and like usual, the bathroom was all steamy.

I wrapped myself in a towel and approached the sink to brush my teeth when I looked up at the steamy mirror and noticed the number two written on it.

I called to my husband to come and see what was on the mirror. We were both stumped. He was adamant that it hadn't been him and we didn't have any children. There was no explanation for it whatsoever.

Those are my experiences of my best friend. I'd like to hope that somehow it was her trying to communicate with me and letting me know that she was okay.

A KISS GOODBYE

When I was sixteen years old, my dad was in for the battle of his life. He had cancer.

About three months into chemo, he had negative results and things were progressing rapidly. I was heartbroken to hear we probably would not have him in our lives much longer.

A month or two after stopping his chemo treatments, he was unexpectedly hospitalized and put onto a ventilator.

My mom was very protective of what my brother and I witnessed about my dad's illness. There were many things that I now know happened, but she had shielded us from. This hospitalization was one of them.

My mom arranged for us to stay with my aunt for a few days while she watched over our father in the hospital. She did call every few hours and had our aunt relay updates to us.

After two days of living with my aunt, and trying my best to pretend everything was alright, my father appeared to me.

It was around eleven o'clock at night and I woke up to the odd feeling that something was watching me.

I was sleeping facing the window, so I slowly rolled over to face the door.

My father was standing at the side of my bed, a loving grin on his face, smiling down at me.

I rubbed my sleepy eyes and told him I was so glad to see him and happy that he was alright and out of the hospital.

He nodded his head, leaned down, kissed me on the forehead and walked out of my room without saying anything.

I didn't think it was strange that he hadn't replied at the time because I was still very groggy.

The next morning, I got ready for school, grabbed my backpack and ran downstairs to the kitchen to grab a quick breakfast before heading out to the bus.

When I'd reached the kitchen, I noticed my entire family was sitting at the dining room table sobbing.

Obviously, because of what had happened the night before, I was in disbelief. I tried to argue with them, telling them that couldn't be because dad was home. I'd seen him last night! In response, I only received sympathetic looks and reassurances that he had truly passed away last night.

My mom and aunt promised me that it had been a dream and only a dream. I knew that I was groggy and half asleep, but I had felt his breath on my forehead when he'd kissed me. It had to have been real.

Now I'm going to take you to another time I encountered my father after his passing.

I was seventeen and my mom and I were fighting. It had ended in me slamming my door and locking myself in my room so I could cry it out.

My radio, which was off at the time, turned on and played my favorite song.

When the song ended, the radio turned itself off.

I checked the connection, the power button and numerous other things to try to explain it. I had no answers. I truly feel like it was my dad trying to comfort me.

When I was eighteen, I had just been dumped by my boyfriend. We had been together for over a year.

In my room, I laid on my bed with swollen eyes, trying to distract myself by watching some television.

My phone chimed and it was from my ex, trying to explain his reasoning for the sudden breakup. Annoyed, I tucked my phone under my pillow.

Just as I had barely laid back down on my bed, a picture of my father and I on my desk fell forward face down. It didn't shatter. I took it as my father trying to get my attention to tell me everything was going to be alright and that he was still here for me.

Although some of my experiences are minor, I find a lot of comfort in the fact that this could have been my father watching over me.

DROPLETS

I had a dream that made my blood run cold. Nothing like this has ever happened to me before in my life.

I love my grandparents dearly, but with a crazy college class schedule to tend to and a part-time job, I was only able to keep in touch with them about once a month.

It was a Thursday night. I had just finished a shift at the local retail store I worked at and I was exhausted. I watched a little tv and then dozed off in bed.

I only remember parts of the dream I had. But what I remember is disturbing enough.

I am standing in an empty parking lot with my grandfather. The moon is almost completely blanketed by clouds and there is one lone streetlight about ten yards away.

From the lack of light, I can make out some of my grandfather's features but not all of them. He is standing about six feet away from me with his head turned towards the black sky, glancing up at the tiny sliver of moon that can be seen.

Suddenly, without notice of thunder or lightning, it just starts pouring rain. I throw my hands above my head in an attempt to shield myself from the droplets. I watch as my grandfather continues to stare up at the sky, rain running down his cheeks and drenching his short white hair.

Finally, after what seems like forever, my grandfather turns to look at me. He blinks rain droplets out of his eyes and smiles, then waves.

I hold my hand up and wave back.

He slowly saunters over to me, scoops me up in a big hug and kisses my forehead.

"You will be fine," he pulls away and searches my face for some sort of understanding.

I look up at him terrified, although I'm not sure why. "Will I be?"

Again, he nods, and rests his chin on the top of my head as we both are inundated by the droplets. "You know you will be."

I burst out into tears that after only a moment or two become hysterical sobs.

He pulls back, puts my chin in his hand and smiles into my eyes before turning and walking in the opposite direction of the streetlamp.

I watch him leave, my stomach lurching with every uncontrollable sob. Once the darkness has swallowed him, I drop to my knees in the pouring rain and cry some more.

At that point, I woke myself up. I was sweating and the dream lingered an echo in my ears.

I lay there in bed, staring at the ceiling, trying to pull myself free from the dream and back to reality. *Everything's ok, I'm ok, grandpa is ok.*

I took a deep breath in, reached for my cell phone and checked the time. My heart stopped as my screen illuminated three missed calls from my grandmother.

I called her back, confused and speechless. She explained that he had passed away in his sleep very suddenly. They thought it was a heart attack.

I fought a lump in my throat that seemed to rise with every word she said. My heart felt like it was being torn in small shreds.

My grandmother hung up and I laid there again, staring at my ceiling. This time, I let the dream wash over me and I cried silent sobs, letting everything sink in.

Had my grandfather come to me in my dreams to say goodbye? To this day, I'm not sure how it was possible, but I think he did.

I FEEL YOU

When I was fourteen, my brother had gone swimming in the local river with some friends from school. It was not a place he was unfamiliar with. We both went there all the time.

Unfortunately, this day there was an accident. My brother was trying to use the rope swing to swing into the river, but when he'd grabbed the rope, it was so wet from the person who had used it before that his hands just slid right off of it. He fell onto the rocks below.

He hadn't died immediately. He was taken by ambulance to the hospital and put into a medically induced coma for two days before we were told he was not going to make it.

For days and months after the funeral, I would just cry and wish I could see or hear him one more time. I missed him so much.

One day, I had just gotten home from school and my mom and dad were both at work as usual. I was usually home alone for about an hour before they arrived on most days.

In our living room, we have one of those love seats that manually recline. I would always sit on the left side and my brother would sit on the right one and we would watch our favorite shows together.

On this specific occasion, I was watching my brother's favorite series. It was an entirely new season that had just started about a week prior.

I had barely started the first episode of the new season and I started to get the munchies, so I paused the show and went to the kitchen to find something good to snack on.

I was rifling through the food pantry when I heard the pop sound of one of the recliner levers being pulled and reclining.

At first, I thought someone might be in the house, so I grabbed the nearest knife, walked to the kitchen doorway and slowly peered around the corner to the living room.

The recliner on my brother's side was fully reclined as if someone was using it. It freaked me out something fierce for a few minutes.

I walked around the house to be sure no one else was in the house, but all the doors were locked and there was no sign of an intruder.

I went back to the kitchen, grabbed a snack, put the knife away and sat back down on the love seat. I gave his chair one last glance, nodded in what I hoped he'd know as recognition and un-paused the show.

I told my parents about what had happened when they got home from work. I was elated to think it could have been my brother. My parents, on the other hand, just dismissed it as a malfunction.

A few months after, I was really having a hard time again, missing my brother to no end.

Again, it was after school before my parents were home and the phone ringed only once before the answering machine clicked on.

I was watching television as usual, reclining away, and then I heard what sounded like my brother's voice saying hello.

I paused my show and listened, and the sound was now gone. Curious, I got up and went to the kitchen to see where the voice was coming from.

I looked down and noticed the red blinking light on the answering machine and pressed play.

It was my brother. There was a ton of static, but you could hear him say "Hello? Hello? Hello?" And then more static and the message ended.

I played the message for my parents when they got home. My dad stepped backwards in shock and my mom turned deathly white. I'm pretty sure after that incident they believed me about my brother possibly reclining the chair.

Since then, I have not heard or seen anything else. I'm still hopeful though.

THE PROMISE RING

When I was seventeen, I was dating a guy who was nineteen. My parents knew about it and, in fact, they loved Sean to death.

Sean did have a motorcycle, which they did not allow me to ride on. Even knowing they didn't want me to ride with him, he'd still ask once in awhile if I wanted to go for a ride.

I don't think it only had to do with the warnings from my parents, but I always had a feeling of dread when he asked me if I wanted to ride it. I just had an overpowering bad feeling. Something in my head just said, *don't do it, don't go.* So, I never did.

I'm really lucky I didn't. Eventually, it is what killed him. It had been raining for weeks, some days pouring massive sheets of rain. Riding a motorcycle was not the safest way to get about.

One rainy morning, I was called to the office at school. I was unsure as to why I was beckoned, because I never did anything to get in trouble.

When I walked into the office, the principal was waiting for me as well as the school psychologist and both of my parents. My mom looked like she had been crying.

At first, I thought someone in my immediate family had died until my dad took my hand in his, sat me down and told me that Sean had passed away in a motorcycle accident.

I was beyond broken. He had been the best thing in my life. He'd even just given me a promise ring two weeks before on my birthday.

After a few weeks, I went back to my part time job at a local craft store. That evening, I had to help close with the manager.

She'd walked me to my car, and then got into her car and was talking on the phone. When I got into my car and was letting it warm up, I had the overwhelming feeling that someone was in the car with me.

I checked the back seat and scanned around the parking lot, but I saw no one else besides my boss, jabbering away in her car on the phone while she slowly backed out of her parking spot.

I shrugged it off as being tired, or maybe just being unnerved because I wasn't used to working this late in the evening.

As I reached down and put my car in reverse, something fell from my mirror.

I put my car in park and turned my interior light on and searched around to find out what could have fallen.

Very recently, I had placed the promise ring Sean had given me on a chain and hung it from my rearview mirror. I found it on the floorboard by my feet with the chain completely intact.

I looked around my car yet again to see no one obviously around. Then, all of the sudden, an overwhelming smell wafted through my car. It was Sean's cologne. It lingered for a minute, maybe two, then subsided.

The next year, when it was barely beginning to warm up to summer weather, I decided to go read my book out by our pool.

I was drinking a soda and lounging on our chaise. I had just turned the page and blindly reached for my can of soda on the table next to me. My fingers did not find cold aluminum, however. It was something different and unexpected.

I placed my book in my lap and turned my attention to the table. There was a lone rose placed on the table right next to my soda. The same roses that were in my mom's garden.

I scanned the backyard for the sign of anyone, to no avail. Then, once again, there was the overwhelming smell of Sean's cologne. It seemed to surround me in an aromatic hug and then faded.

I sat there in shock on the chaise, staring intently at my mom's prized rose bushes and the few stems that seemed to waver in the wind. Except there was no wind.

DRIFTING OFF

My mother Elena suffered from epilepsy. She had it as long as I could remember. Now grown and on my own, I felt it was my duty to take her in and keep an eye on her. You never knew when she would have a seizure and there's no known cure for it.

Some people are lucky and only have it occur for a few years, while others have it their entire lives. My mom was an unfortunate case.

It was around two in the morning, and a clatter coming from my mother's room woke me up.

Hastily, I ran to investigate. My mother was tangled in her bedding, obviously having a seizure and suffocating. I did my best to untangle her while dialing 911.

I performed CPR on her until paramedics arrived. Once they were in the house, I felt like I was in an ant farm. People were running here and shuffling there. I was shoved out of the way so they could work on her. I was numb. Delirious and numb.

I sat on the bottom stair, which was right outside her bedroom, and just stared off into space. The only thought I could recollect is *this better not be how it ends. This cannot be how it ends.*

After a few minutes, which almost felt like hours, paramedics got her breathing again. Immediately, they transported her to the hospital.

I stayed behind to get dressed. I was still in my boxers with no shirt on.

In my room, still numb, fumbling through my drawers for something quick and easy to throw on, the phone rang. It was my aunt.

I answered thoughtlessly, still exhausted.

She was breathless and sounded groggy. "Jake, you will not believe the dream I just had. I had a dream that I was on a boat with your mother. We were sailing off into the golden bright sunset and then she turned to me and told me she was dead. It felt so real."

I choked on her words and just sat there in silence. I stared at the wall in front of me. I knew. Well, I was pretty sure I knew. This was too much of a coincidence to not have some truth.

I told her what had just happened, and she agreed to meet me at the hospital immediately.

I tugged on my shoes, grabbed my keys and drove in a blur to the hospital.

As I expected, the doctor was waiting for me when I arrived. His facial expression told me all I needed to know. She was gone.

The chaplain escorted my Aunt and I to a room and to console us. I know I was supposed to feel better after talking with him, but I didn't.

I sat there with my elbows on my knees, my head in my hands and tried to stay calm. I tried to make sense of the words being directed at me. But I felt like I was trying to understand Charlie Brown's teacher. None of it made much sense.

I didn't get home until around six in the morning. The horizon was already peeking light throughout the valley.

I threw my keys in my key dish and landed with a belly-flop on the couch. There was no need to sleep in my bed, this would do just fine.

I grabbed the blanket off of the back of the couch and tucked myself under it, as if hiding from the world would shield the pain I was feeling. The absolute shock and loss were overwhelming my entire body.

Soon I drifted off. I dreamt of an ocean. The water's edge was highlighted by golden sunlight. It was beautiful.

Birds cawed in the distance and the lapping noises of the ocean were soothing. I was on a boat. *The* boat. My Aunt's boat.

My mom sat next to me smiling, watching me be mesmerized by the water and the sky. She put the back of her hand up and grazed my cheek.

"I guess you know," she said and stared off into the sunset.

"I guess I know," I replied.

OFF THE ROAD

My mom passed away from cancer. It wasn't a surprise. We watched her struggle to beat it for years. But finally, it had taken over everything and there was nothing left to fight.

My paranormal story begins at the age of twelve. The house felt like emptiness. There wasn't a room you could walk into that wasn't heavy with underlying depression or pain.

No one was sleeping well. None of us had much of an appetite either. We just... lived. We went about our days until the funeral mostly like zombies.

You wouldn't dare mention the upcoming funeral for fear my father would break down into a sobbing pile on the floor. With my sister, every time anyone spoke to her, she ran off sobbing and slammed her bedroom door. We were an absolute depressive mess of a family.

On the day of the funeral was when it happened. It was time for us to get on with our lives and pull out of this dark hole of grief. I wonder if it was my mom shaking us back into reality or something -- like we needed a wakeup call.

After the funeral, my father was driving us home. All of our eyes were swollen and stinging. Our nerves were on edge and our hearts were numb.

I remember looking out the window as we drove. Seeing a certain store or recognizing a road sign, I thought to myself about the many times I had driven past these landmarks with my mom in the car. There would no longer be a mom in my life, let alone in the car with me. Then it happened.

My dad swears he didn't fall asleep at the wheel. He said something ran across the road. But no one found evidence of anything running across the road or being hit.

The car swerved and smack into a tree. I was ejected from the vehicle. For moments or minutes, I was out.

When I came to, I heard a truck blaring its horn and someone pulling me by my arms out of the road. The sun was glaring right into my eyes, but I could have sworn it was my mom.

She looked happy. And healthy. Like mom again. The mom I hadn't had in my life for several years.

I remember, amongst the pain in my shoulder and the road rash on my side, an absolute feeling of tranquility. It was as if an aura of healing, warmth and so much love just emitted off of her and on to me. Then, everything went black again.

I woke up in the hospital. My father had been pinned in the car but only broken a leg. My sister had a minor concussion. I on the other hand, had a fractured collarbone, dislocated shoulder and some pretty substantial road rash on my entire left side of my body. I was lucky. It could have been much worse.

A long-haul truck had been driving along the road where we crashed and, because the accident occurred on a curve, he hadn't had time to stop right away.

Paramedics talked to me briefly at the scene, most of which was a complete blur because I was in and out of consciousness. I told them about my mom and her pulling me off of the road. As a result, the first responders had searched the woods for her, thinking she must have been thrown from the car as well.

It wasn't until my dad spoke to them that they stopped searching. They figured I was in shock because we had just left my mother's funeral.

The odd thing is that, while I would like to believe it was a dream, the truck driver described to police that a woman pulled me off of the road right before he would have hit me. I read the report. And he described my mom, down to the dress we buried her in. So, you tell me. Did my mom pull me off of that road and save my life?

CREAKING

I've been living in this town for about two years now. For the last year or so, I've been feeling a strange uneasiness when I'm in my house, but also when I'm just out and about in town, almost as though it's following me.

At night, I usually hear the sound of my floorboards creaking, as though there is someone walking across the floor, even when I'm alone in the house. I've seen shadows and dark silhouettes on my walls, even when there is no light to produce them, and I've heard things banging on my doors and from inside of the cupboard in my room, when I'm certain nothing could be causing it. All of this activity has been happening since I moved in, in recurring intervals. There hasn't been a moment where it's stopped for more than a short period of time.

Ever since I was little, I've had this feeling of being watched by something I could never see. These feelings of uneasiness have haunted me even before I moved into this house, although it had never been as bad as it is now. I remember having terrible nightmares when I was younger, and I would often wake up screaming in the middle of the night, terrified of something I couldn't see. The nightmares only got worse over time.

So, in general, I've had strange experiences my whole life, though I've never really understood what any of it was.

Back to the present, a friend of mine has been having strange experiences of her own. She used to be a big fan of dolls and has grown up around them since she was a baby. It's only recently that she has lost her love for them and is trying to sell them off. But there is one particular doll that has, undoubtedly, a creepy aura around her. Something just feels off about her, and my friend recently told me that she has seen the doll moving on its own. On a few occasions, she's even seen the doll peeking its head around her bedroom door to watch her sleep, and the doll has sometimes been heard screaming and wailing for no apparent reason (and it shouldn't even be able to make sound).

For the past week or so, I've been looking after this doll. The room where my friend has been keeping all the dolls, she's selling is getting too cramped (this one is a pretty big doll), and she told me she wanted a break from all the disruption that the doll has been causing her, so I offered to look after it for a few days. The doll has been staying in my room since then, and while I was beginning to doubt there was anything wrong with it after all, that changed a few days ago.

I decided to set up the camera on my phone to record the doll while I wasn't in my room, just on the off chance I caught her doing anything *out of the ordinary*. To my disappointment, she didn't move at all in the video I took. But after watching it half a dozen times, I paid careful attention to her face, and noticed that at the start of the video, just as I left to go downstairs and turned off the light, her eye went blood red (her normal eye colour is bluey-green). When I came back up, half an hour later, to check on her, her eye was back to its normal colour.

Two nights before this, I had woken up in the middle of the night to the feeling of something pressing me down into my bed. At the time, it had been too dark to see what or who it was. When I tried to turn my bedside light on, so that I could see, I couldn't move my arms. They were being held down by something. What creeped me out the most, however, was the feeling of hair dangling down onto my face. My legs felt numb, and for some reason they were too heavy to lift. I couldn't move anything. It didn't help that, at the time, I was ill and feeling physically quite weak and tired. I fear that my weakness made me an easy target for whatever was in my house at that time.

I don't remember what happened afterwards, but at some point, I must have fallen back asleep.

When I woke up the next morning, I discovered an ugly bruise on my arm that hadn't been there before, in the exact same place where I had been held down. I was pretty shaken up by the experience, and I immediately told my friend what had happened. She was just as freaked out as I was.

Any time my friend or I look at the doll, it almost feels as though the energy is being drained from our bodies. It renders me physically weak and tired. While my friend has been feeling like that for years, this is a first for me. And now I'm certain that there's something wrong with the doll after all.

SHARDS OF GLASS

The day was Wednesday, 21st February 2018. I had been fighting a cold that wouldn't go for the past two months, and that evening I fixed myself some medication. I carried a glass of water to my room to take the meds with, and once I was finished, I put the glass down on the chest of drawers by my bed. The drawers themselves weren't very height, and my room had a thick carpet.

During the night, I was woken up suddenly to the sound of glass shattering. The noise startled me, and I laid there with my heart thudding in my chest, wondering what I had heard. I started to think I had merely dreamt the noise, since the house was so still and silent. After a few minutes of trying to calm myself down and hearing nothing else, I eventually went back to sleep.

The next thing that woke me up was my alarm, the following morning. I turned it off and swung my legs over the bed, putting my feet down to where my flip flops were waiting (where I had left them the night before). I had my feet in the shoes before I reached out to switch the lamp on, since it was still pretty dark. As soon as the light came on, I was overcome with an intense feeling of shock.

Less than half an inch from my right foot was the base of a shattered glass. The same one I had put on the table last night, after taking my medicine. There was an incredibly sharp piece of glass sticking up from the carpet, almost like an inverted dagger, right next to my ankle. The base of the glass was upright next to it, and all of the glass had completely shattered, laying around it.

What unnerved me the most was how it had happened. It didn't make any sense to me. There was no plausible explanation for why the glass would have moved off the chest of drawers by itself and shattered on the thick carpet in such a way that all the shards had landed around the base. Never mind that single piece of glass that was sticking up towards me.

Being careful to avoid the glass, I went and told my mom what had happened. That's when she told me that something weird had happened to her during the night as well. She said that she'd woken up at some point to the feeling that someone had crawled onto the bed with her and had pinned her down. She told me she was still half-dreaming at the time, but when she looked up, she was staring at the grotesque, mangled face of a little girl. She said it was horrible to look at, and she was sure that whatever this thing was, it was malicious and wanted to hurt her. Because she was still semi-asleep, she began to dream that I had walked into the room, and the face of the little girl changed into that of a normal, pretty child. Then as soon as I left, the face changed again to become ugly and grotesque. The girl – or whatever it was – shook her around the bed for a few minutes, before it finally left. She was so freaked out. By the time the thing started shaking her, she was completely awake and aware of what was happening. After that, she barely slept for the next five days, terrified it would happen again.

I began to notice scratches appearing on my arms too. They were thin and jagged, almost like cat scratches, even though we don't have any pets. On the following Thursday and Friday, I also noticed strange red marks appearing on my neck, like pressure marks that just wouldn't go away. I knew for certain that nobody was anywhere near my room at the time, so I have no idea what could have caused them.

I tried asking one of my friends for help and explained to him everything that had happened. He told me that it sounded like someone had brought something dark into the house, and whatever it was had somehow fixated on me. I thought that my mom had gotten off much worse though, so I didn't understand how it could be attached to me.

NOT ALONE AT ALL

A new chapter in my life had begun. I was officially a homeowner, really, I had been so for nearly a month now, but the house hadn't yet truly felt like it was quite mine yet. With the table in my trunk, I would be putting the finishing touches on the decor that would transform the house from an empty shell to my home.

I turned onto my street and drove about halfway down the block to where I now lived. Even after a month I still had yet to meet any of my neighbors, not officially anyways. It wasn't like they weren't close by, they just seemed to keep their distance only giving me sideways glances or peeking at me from behind their partially drawn curtains. It didn't bother me though, some communities were very close, and it took time to break into their circles, I had plenty of time.

Once I drove into the garage, I unloaded the table and hauled it into the house pressing the button to close the garage door on the way in. The spot that the table would go had already been picked out and cleared so it didn't take me too long to get it situated and my personal possessions set atop its surface.

I appreciated my work with the table, it appeared just as I had imagined in my head when I first discovered it for sale online. I still couldn't get over how I had picked it up for only $50. Things like this could cost you thousands of dollars and the person seemed either not to know what they had or were just looking for a quick sale. I had felt a little guilty when I had left with my treasure, but the man had been adamant about getting rid of it, his loss and my gain I suppose.

The rest of the day was very quiet, consisting of watching some light cleaning, eating dinner and watching of some television, basically the average night for me. Sometime around 9:30 I was getting tired and decided to turn in for the evening.

I had just turned down the covers on my bed and went to the bathroom to brush my teeth when I heard what sounded like footsteps walking through the halls. I quickly turned off the sink to allow me to hear better but as soon as the water went off the sound seemed to stop completely. Shrugging I assumed it might be a loose pipe somewhere and resolved to call a plumber the next day to have it checked out.

Oddly enough, the noise didn't seem to start back up when I turned the knob on the sink once more but in the month that I had been there already I'd never heard anything amiss. Finishing up my bathroom routine I climbed into bed and prepared to go to sleep. That's when the footsteps started again.

I was supposed to be alone in the house, so the sound of footsteps sent a chill down my spine. I tried to convince myself that it was just the house settling in its foundation or the residual movement of the pipe from the bathroom, but I knew better, it was definitely someone walking.

The movement seemed to be coming from the living room where I had been just a few minutes before. The thought that someone had been here the entire evening watching me whilst I was unaware was even more disturbing than the idea that someone had broken into my home.

Now that I was sure I wasn't alone the question was what I was going to do about it? Do I stay quiet and hide someone in the house or do I confront my intruder?

My mind screamed for me to hide but I wasn't about to allow someone to stain my thoughts of my new home. It probably wasn't the best option to give away my presence but after the words left my mouth there was no taking them back. "Hello? Is someone there?"

I thought that I had surprised whoever was out there when the walking stopped suddenly. "I'm going to call the police, so you'd better leave right now!" I yelled suddenly emboldened.

With that the walking started coming in my direction. Knowing the threat, I'd made was a mistake I grabbed the edge of my covers trying to hide from whoever was coming towards me. Every creak of the floorboard brought them closer and closer. A knot of fear constricted in my stomach as I saw the beginning of a shadow come into view through my door.

I wanted to close my eyes, hoping that shielding my eyes would somehow protect me. I strained to close them, but I was unable to pull my gaze from the opening. The shadow stretched farther on the wall and the sound of the steps were getting louder and louder. A couple more steps and they would be outside my door. I tried to take a breath, but I felt like I was choking on the air itself.

I heard one, two, three more steps and the shadow seemed to pass by my door without someone appearing, yet the sound seemed to have moved on by continuing down the hallway. Had I missed them? Had they missed me? Neither option seemed very likely.

I slid my way out from under the covers and stood on unsteady legs. Slowly I made my way to the door, every step of my own seemed to sound a hundred times louder than it probably was. I kept reminding myself that this was my house and I had to protect it. I tried to find some sort of weapon to protect myself, but nothing stood out that would do much good. I would just have to hope that the other person didn't have a gun or a knife.

Whoever it was seemed to have stopped at the end of the hall. I edged around the frame of the door trying to get a peek at my assailant, but the shadows concealed them from view. The element of surprise was on their side as long as the lights were off. I had to do something to change the balance. The switch for the hall was a few steps away, if I could just make it there before they realized what I planned to do then maybe I could take them by surprise, even scare them off in doing so.

I steady my legs and rushed forward. As soon as I left the room, I heard footsteps pounding down the hall in pursuit of me. My hands shook as I fumbled with the switch sure that it was too late, that I had botched my chance.

Moments before the intruder was on me, I flipped the lights on and turned expecting them to crash into me. Instead, I was met by an empty hallway, I was alone.

The idea that everything that had happened was in my head seemed impossible. Sure, I was alone here but I wasn't crazy. The sounds had been unmistakable, someone else was here. I made my way down to the end of the hall hoping to catch someone hiding there. The only place someone could be in the guestroom at the end of the hall.

The door was closed so I flung the door open as hard and as fast as I could. "Who's there?" I yelled.

A cold gust of air seemed to blow past me causing me to look towards the window expecting to see it open where someone had escaped. The thing was though that the window was shut and upon inspection locked. That left only one place for someone to be: the closet.

Angrier than scared at this point I marched over to the door and flung it open ready to put an end to this game. Nothing.

There was no way someone could have gotten by me undetected, so I was at a loss. I stood there, turning in a slow circle trying to see if I could have overlooked something to no effect. There was most definitely no one but me in the room. Then they started again, the footsteps, moving down the hall towards the living room, it was as if whoever was there was mocking me, by being so obvious about their presence.

As I made my way out the door the sound of something crashing to the ground removed any doubt that I hadn't been imagining the whole thing. I quickened my pace, pushing myself forward. Exiting the hall, I saw my new table laying on its side, the things I had placed upon it scattered on around the floor.

It had only been a few seconds, yet the room was empty and the sound of someone walking had stopped.

Looking over my belongings it didn't appear that anything was broken, even the table seemed to have suffered no damage. Reaching down to pick it up I noticed the underside of it for the first time. Strange symbols had been carved into the wood, symbols I didn't recognize. Just the sight of them sent a chill down my spine.

Wanting to put the odd markings out of view I righted the table and arranged the ornamentations back in their respective positions. Still, I couldn't get the image of those markings out of my head.

I searched the entirety of the house but found no trace of anyone there but myself. The rest of the night was quiet, no footsteps came, and sometime after 1:00 exhaustion overcame my unease and I fell asleep.

Over the next few days there were a number of occasions where I would find the things on top of the table seemed to have been brushed off its surface or the table itself being knocked over just as it had been the first evening I had brought it home. I tried to ignore the thoughts that were creeping into my head that were telling me something had come into my home with it. I'd heard of objects having things attached to them, but I refused to believe that is what was going on even though there wasn't really any other explanation.

Finally, after nearly a week, I couldn't take it anymore, the table had to go. I packed it back into my car and took it to a second-hand store where I could leave it as a donation. Immediately after returning home, it felt as if a lightness had come over the house. Whatever energy was attached to that table was removed when I took the table out. I just hope it doesn't find its way back.

BEYOND THE ENTRANCE

The crunching sound of sticks and leaves snapping under my boots was the only sound that broke up the silence of the forest. I had been making my way along the worn dirt pathway that snaked its way through the trees disappearing and reappearing from view between the trunks.

The ground was relatively flat making the trek easy enough for an experienced hiker like myself. The trial continued on further, winding its way up the side of one of the small hills. My initial intention was to follow the established route further up the hill for a mile or so before retracing the way back from which I came.

I paused and grabbed the bottle at my waist to take a small swallow of water before starting my way up. As I raised it to my lips, I caught sight of a small outcrop of rock jutting out the side of the hill a little way off the trail.

In no hurry to be anywhere that day I left the trail and zigzagged my way between the trees towards the formation. As I got closer the beginning of the opening to a natural cave came into view. I'd been up here nearly a dozen times before without noticing it and seeing how close it was to the trail it took me by surprise.

Going into a place such as a cave isn't always a good idea in the woods since there can be any number of animals that call them home. Standing at the mouth I squinted attempting to have my eyes penetrate the dark interior with little success.

Attempting to startle anything that might be hiding inside I decided to shout into the opening. "Hello! Is anyone in there?"

The only thing that came back was a slight

echo of my own voice. An echo meant that the cave was much larger than the small opening suggested. My sense of adventure felt like a physical force pushing me forward, but something had me hesitating. With no light on me I knew an extended exploration was going to be impossible but that didn't mean I couldn't check out the first few feet where daylight still allowed me to see.

My mind made up I made one final attempt to see inside. The moment's hesitation brought with it something that I didn't expect. The hairs on the back of my neck stood on end and a shiver passed up and down my spine that ended as a flutter in my gut. Whether it was real or imagined I felt a cold drip of sweat trail its way down my neck and down my back.

In a moment the darkness inside changed causing me to unconsciously take a couple of steps away. No sound had come from the space in front of me but somehow, I just knew something was there even though I couldn't see it.

"Hello?" I intended for my voice to sound

strong by shouting louder than I had before, but it came out as a high-pitched squeak that cracked halfway through. Anyone or anything that was inside most definitely could hear the fear impregnated within the single word.

I was greeted again by only an echo and a lengthy moment of silence. Somehow, I was able to convince myself that what I felt simply was my mind playing tricks on me. It was only a cave after all. So, I gathered what courage I possessed and ducked into the small opening.

The surface of the walls seemed to dance as the sun cast my shadow along the rough rock. After a few feet the cave opened up into a larger chamber, most of which was hidden in darkness since the sun's rays quickly dissolved after only a few feet. Without a light the cave wall could only be a few feet in front of me or thousands...

Somewhere off to one side I hear a shuffling sound coming towards me. Fear prickles along my scalp as I imagine an animal coming towards me. Worst case scenarios start flashing through my head as I see myself getting torn apart by any number of carnivores. I try to make my feet move, to retreat back the way I came but every muscle in my body is frozen.

Whatever is coming towards me is right on top of me when the cave goes silent. The only sound comes from the shuddering breaths I take as I fight to regain control of myself. Seconds tick by one by one, each seemingly longer than the next.

I'm nearly convinced I'm alone, that the sounds were just in my head when a voice from the void around me turns the blood in my veins to ice.

"I'm alone..." it said to me. With the words came an overwhelming sense of misery. I felt like I was drowning in it. Wave after wave crashed down on me making it impossible to feel anything but the unending sense of isolation and loneliness. I'd never experienced anything even close to this, every moment threatened to drive me over the edge.

Just as quickly as it came on it was over. At some point I had fallen to the floor of the cave. Tears continued to stream unchecked down my face to pool unseen on the stone beneath me.

Getting up proved to be more difficult than expected. I was completely drained both physically and emotionally. I half crawled half stumbled my way out of the cave, led out only by the light from the sun beyond.

I'm not sure what that was inside the cave. Frankly I'm not interested in going back to investigate further. To this day that trail is one that I have avoided exploring since that day. I truly believe I came into contact with the spirit of someone who died in that cave, alone and scared. In the moment when it spoke to me, I think I felt what they did, alone and scared, energy remaining from a tragic death.

IT BURNED ME

Twilight had come and darkness was settling in for the evening. The four of us had drawn the curtains across the windows of my bedroom further darkening the scene, a dark place for dark intentions. Shadows danced on the walls of my bedroom as the flames licked at the wax of the freshly lit candles.

In the dim light I make out the faces of my friends who agreed to be here tonight. We sit in a circle around the Ouija board, the planchette resting atop it. As anxious as I was before, now I'm having second thoughts as to the wisdom of what we're doing. It's as if touching the small indicator would mean crossing a threshold in which there was no return. My best friend Allison who is sitting to my right appears to be battling her own apprehension by the way she held her hands against her chest.

My friend Alexis who initially suggested this is the first to finally make the first move to touch the teardrop shaped pointer. "Are we going to do this or what?" Her eyes meet each of ours in a silent challenge.

"This is stupid, I mean it's obviously fake." Trina, the last girl in the room, would have been more convincing if her voice hadn't shaken when she said it.

"If it's fake then what's the harm in trying it?" Alexis said.

"Amanda, you're telling me you actually believe this? I mean it's just plastic and cardboard..." Trina asks looking in my direction.

I know that the two of them could argue for an hour and not sway the other to their side, so I made a decision for them. I let out a sigh and set my fingers on the planchette. "Come on, let's just do this."

The debate over Allison and Trina joined their fingers with my own and Alexis's on the device. "So how does this work? Are we supposed to ask questions or something?" I asked.

Alexis being the self-appointed leader of this ritual glanced at a piece of paper she had sitting next to her and quickly answered. "It says here that we have to state we are open to communication from any entity that is present and has something they want to say. Then we just wait for a response."

Shuffling to another page she began reading off some words she had found on the internet that was supposed to open a link to any spirits nearby. Allison tried to stifle a giggle while Trina on the other hand made no attempt to stop the exaggerated roll of her eyes.

I shot them both a look of disapproval before turning back to the board. "So, what should we ask? Maybe if there is anyone there?"

"It's as good a start as any," Alexis said with a shrug.

She spoke our question out loud to the dark room. The four of us held our collective breath in anticipation, our eyes boring a hole into the pointer. The seconds ticked on until the waiting became uncomfortable with the planchette remaining motionless.

I pushed checking to make sure it wasn't stuck on something. It moved freely back and forth without issue. I was about to suggest that we give up, that it wasn't going to work when the planchette suddenly stopped. I pushed harder trying to get it to slide as before but no matter how hard I pressed I couldn't get it to budge.

"Is that any of you? Cuz it's not funny."

The only response I got was my friends shaking their heads that they weren't doing anything. They each in turn tried to push themselves but were unable to get it to move either.

I was getting really freaked out at this point

and just wanted to put the board away. "I think I've had enough fun with this thing for one night."

All of us removed our fingers and I reached out to pick up the planchette so we could put the board back in the box. I pulled but it was as if someone had taken glue and fastened it to the board. No matter how hard I tried it wouldn't come off. Out of nowhere a searing pain started from my fingertips and moved all the way to my shoulder.

"Ow!" Both the shock and the pain itself made me drop the board and clutch my hand protectively to my chest.

Allison edged closer to me. "Are you okay? What happened?"

I looked down to the object in question. It had fallen face up, the arrow still stuck where it had been before. I sat staring down at it unsure of what had just happened. "It burned me."

"It what?"

I shake my hand trying to ease some of the lingering pain to no effect. "It felt like I got burned." I repeated myself.

"But that's not... possible." Trina said.

A scraping noise draws my attention down to the floor. Even though none of us are touching the planchette it is moving slowly across the board. All of us stare down at it in disbelief as it edges its way towards the place on the board that said: GOODBYE.

It stopped briefly then the planchette flew across the room and slammed against the wall. The flames on the candles sputtered slightly as if a gust of wind had blown through the room even though none of us had felt anything.

Allison was the first to let out an ear-splitting scream and run for the door and out into the hallway. The rest of us in our haste to follow nearly toppled the still-lit candles onto the floor. Even though I didn't look back I could feel something right behind me, gaining on me even as I raced down the hall and away from my room.

It wasn't until I reached the living room that I risked a glance back over my shoulder. A dark shadow seemed to be creeping back sulking back from where we had just come.

Huddled together on the couch we sat there the rest of the night, unwilling to fall asleep fearing whatever it was we contacted with the board might come back.

The following day I took the Ouija board and burned it. After the experience of the night before I was unwilling to keep something in my house that had the power to bring something like that to me. I just hope that getting rid of the board itself is enough to remove whatever come through.

THE HAUNTING OF REDBURN MANOR

SNEAK PEAK

(A HORROR NOVEL – APRIL 2021)

Prologue

Hey, you recording yet?"

Randall grunted, still fiddling with the laptop as he set up the live stream. "Give me a minute," he muttered. "Wifi's being slow."

Nathan clicked his tongue impatiently, glancing at the others. "You know what to do?"

Avery rolled her eyes. "How long have we been doing this?"

"Alright, alright. Just making sure," Nathan said, holding out his hands defensively. "Lucy can kick us off, yeah?"

"Sure!"

"Alright, and we're live in 3... 2... 1."

"Hey there, ghost streamers," Lucy started, her voice echoing faintly around the open dining room. "What an exciting end to our investigation. We've caught a ton of evidence here that we're super excited to share with you."

Nathan nodded, chiming in: "Bixbee Mansion has been a place long renowned in the history books for its tragic past, and during our stay we got a glimpse of what it must have been like living here."

"Don't forget, all of the evidence we captured will be uploaded onto our website for you to look at, so let us know your thoughts in the comments. Did we capture evidence of paranormal activity at Bixbee Mansion?" Randall said cryptically, grinning at the camera. "I think you'll be pretty impressed with what we got."

Lucy shuffled the notes in her hand, taking her cue from Nathan. "Alright then, let's start with a little history lesson on Bixbee Mansion, before we get into the meat of the investigation," she said. "The house was built in the early 1800s by one Henry Bixbee, a man we actually know very little about. The house's early history is somewhat difficult to find, but it stayed in the Bixbee family until the early 1900s. During the first World War, it was actually used as a hospital to support the excessive number of injured soldiers, and so these rooms witnessed a lot of illness and death. Many soldiers died here due to their wounds, and some of that negative energy still lingers today. A man named Rupert Thompson is one of those whose spirit is said to haunt the mansion, and some of the evidence we caught suggests that we managed to make contact with him. Randall, do you want to play that?"

Randall nodded, fiddling with the audio on the laptop and playing the EVP they had recorded on their second night of investigation.

"Can you tell us your name?" Avery's voice came through on the audio, slightly muffled against the background static.

A few moments later, there was a faint whisper, clear enough to distinguish a man's voice. "Rupert."

"Did you die here?"

Again, there was crackly silence for a while, and then another whisper, slightly broken up. "Bu…llet."

Randall stopped the audio and Lucy glanced back down at her notes. "Rupert Thompson died from a severe shrapnel wound after many days of suffering alone in one of the temporary hospital rooms. We also managed to record an EVP of a child speaking to us. We unearthed in our records that the original Henry Bixbee had a niece called Lily, who died here from poor health in 1821. It may be possible that it was her voice we captured during our investigation."

She flicked a glance at Randall, who pulled up the second audio file with a few clicks of the laptop.

"Did you used to live here?" This time it was Nathan's voice asking the question.

There was a soft whine of static.

"Were you here when the house was a hospital?"

Then a child's spoke in a low, harsh whisper. "Bad... place..."

Randall stopped the audio. "We hear the child saying 'bad place' in this clip, though we're not entirely sure what she might be referring to. We later uncovered the secret that Lily's illness might not have been entirely accidental, either. Henry's brother, and Lily's father, was known to be a cruel man who didn't much care for his wife and daughter. While this is mostly speculation, given the child's warning of the house being a 'bad place', it is possible that something more sinister happened here during the residence of the Bixbee family."

Nathan picked up then, talking about some of the experiences he'd had during the stay. "During the second night, I actually had something tug on the back on my shirt. We replayed the clip several times, and there's nothing in the environment that could have caused it."

"During our three day stay here," Avery finished up, "we've collected a range of evidence. And we think it's safe to say that Bixbee Mansion lives up to its haunted reputation. Is it possible the ghost of Lily Bixbee and Rupert Thompson, as well as countless other soldiers, reside here after their deaths? We think so."

"And that's it from us today. This is Avery, Lucy, Nate and Randall, coming at you live from Bixbee Mansion. Stay tuned for next week's episode, where we'll be investigating a house that has seen over two hundred years of murder, suicide and death."

Chapter
ONE

The car skidded to a stop with a sudden lurch, and something thudded against the floor of the trunk. Avery jerked forward in her seat, catching herself against the headrest in front of her, and shot John, their driver, a narrow look.

The man smiled sheepishly, brushing a piece of curling grey hair away from his face. "Sorry," he said. "Hope none of your equipment got damaged."

"I'm sure it's fine," Nathan said with a dismissive wave, unclipping his seat belt. "Thanks for the ride. You remember when you're picking us up?"

"End of the week," John said. "Friday."

Nathan nodded and reached over to open his door. In the back, Randall, Lucy and Avery groaned and stretched as they shuffled out of the car. They'd spent the two hour car journey squashed together with their luggage that couldn't fit in the trunk.

Avery stretched her arms over her head, hearing her shoulder joints pop. "Glad that's over," she muttered, going round the back of the car to help Randall unload the bags.

Nathan propped his hands on his hips with a mystified look on his face. "I thought the journey was fine. Pretty comfy if you ask me."

The three of them shot him a look, and he cowered with a grin. "Alright, alright, you can fight over the front seat next time."

Hauling their bags onto the pavement beside the car, Randall shut the trunk and they waved John off as he pulled away, saluting them in the wing mirror.

"Well, this is it," Lucy said. "We're here."

Nathan nodded at the house in front of them. "Redburn Manor, in all her beauty."

"More like fallen splendour," Lucy muttered, scanning her eyes over the grimy brown bricks, spiderwebbed with cracks and dirt. Ivy tumbled down one side of the house, pushing through the bricks with its long, spindly tendrils.

"There's a certain charm to it," Randall said with a shrug. "What do you think, Avery?"

The three of them turned to her, and she dragged her eyes away from the upper window, where she'd been staring. "Charming, yeah," she said distractedly.

"Well, shall we get inside then?" Nathan said, producing an old-fashioned key from his pocket.

"Lead the way."

It was already late in the afternoon by the time they'd arrived at the house, and although the air was warmed from the sun, grey clouds were banking in from the west, burgeoning with rain, and a chill had begun to blow, stirring leaves across the pavement.

Redburn Manor was a shadow blotted against the sky. An old, crumbling husk of something that was once grand and beautiful. It was a three-story building, with ornate turreted windows that now seemed drab and gloomy in the shade, the glass dirty and cracked in places.

As Nathan slid the key into the lock, Avery almost held her breath.

The door opened without a noise. Particles of disturbed dust flew up, glinting in the wavering light of the afternoon. Nathan shot the others a glance over his shoulder before being the first to step inside. Randall followed, then Lucy.

Avery waited another few seconds before she too stepped forward. From where she was stood, the entryway stretched down into semi-darkness. The sunlight that had been warming her back before dipped behind one of those dark clouds, and the wind stirred strands of hair across her face.

"You coming?" Lucy asked, glancing over her shoulder when she noticed Avery hadn't followed.

Schooling her features into a more casual pose, she nodded and stepped in after them.

The sensation of dust on her skin was the first thing she noticed; it itched along her arms and tickled the back of her throat, making her cough. The place had been shut up for a long time, after its last stint as a Bed and Breakfast a few years ago. After the last tragedy happened, the place sunk into its own despair, becoming a place nobody cared for anymore.

"Woah!" Randall said from further inside. "This place is huge!" His voice echoed along the high-vaulted ceiling, stirring the cobwebs that latticed the rafters. There was a staircase on the left, which stretched up into darkness, and on her right, an old-fashioned mirror with gilded edges that was obscured by dust and old fingerprints.

Lucy ran a finger along its edge, pulling away a streak of muck.

"Back when it was a Bed and Breakfast, this place was able to accommodate up to twenty people," she said as she used the sleeve of her jacket to wipe away some of the dirty prints on the glass. Avery watched the reflection clear, showing her the staircase on the opposite side. Mirrors were often said to hold a lot of spiritual energy, and she made a note to keep an eye on it.

"I thought it was a hotel?" Randall said.

"That was before it became a Bed and Breakfast. Neither businesses lasted very long."

"And before any of that, it served as a mental institution," Nathan added, his teeth flashing in the dark.

The rest of them shared a glance, half-uncertain smiles creeping along their faces. Places like mental institutions and hospitals – where people were usually sick and not very well cared for – were often imbued with negative energies far more than other buildings. Emotions like fear and grief and anger could be soaked up by old houses, continuing to manifest in such ways for years to come.

On the street outside, they all heard the rumble of a car engine, and the faint squeal of tires as it pulled up against the curb.

"That'll be Caroline," Lucy said, breaking the silence. "I'll go see if she needs any help with her bags."

Lucy disappeared back outside, while Avery lingered behind the other two, taking in every detail of the entryway. She could feel the weight of the house's grandeur, even amongst the dust and shadows. She figured this must have been a beautiful house once, home to an aristocratic family. But then it had been sold off and adopted into a temporary mental institution in the late 1800s and early 1900s. That's when its real history begins as a place synonymous with tragic death and suicide. The reason they were there, investigating the rumours and stories that had been shared over the years.

"Where do you want to set up base?" Nathan asked as he poked his head into the door on his right, pulling away with a sniff. "Ugh, this place hasn't been cleaned in years."

"Wherever has the least dust," Randall said with a shrug.

The door behind them opened again, shedding watery grey light into the landing. Avery noticed for the first time the hummingbirds printed on the wallpaper. In the strange light, they looked too thin and lanky.

"Hi guys," Caroline said as she came through, brushing aside a strand of pale yellow hair.

"Hey Carol," Nathan said, lifting his hand. "Good journey?"

"Yeah, traffic wasn't too bad," she said absently, lugging a bag after her and setting it down by her feet with a huff.

"Next time, I'm travelling with you," Randall muttered, shaking his head. "John's driving is getting worse."

Caroline chuckled, and Lucy came in after her with another black bag strung around her shoulder.

"What have you got in here?" She said, struggling to lower it to the floor.

"Psychic things," she said with a wink, chuckling. "I like to come prepared, that's all."

"Let's get set up and do an introductory session," Nathan suggested, leading the group further into the house. Passing the room

Nathan had glanced in before, Avery paused to peer inside. Although the curtains were open, there wasn't much light in the room, and it was heavy with the scent of mildew. Old, rotted furniture and moth-eaten sheets and not much else.

She pulled away, throwing a smile at Caroline over her shoulder, and followed the two men into the large sitting room at the end of the hall.

"Looks cosy. Want to set up our equipment in here?"

"Sure."

Randall lugged a black duffel bag onto the coffee table beside an ornate fireplace, being careful not to be too heavy handed. Their equipment was expensive, and they probably couldn't afford replacements if anything got damaged.

Avery looked around in awe, admiring the decorated ceiling panels and the silver-edged chandelier suspended from the middle of the room. "Must've been one posh Bed and Breakfast," she muttered to nobody in particular. "I'm surprised all this stuff is still here."

"Well, after what happened to the previous owners, I guess nobody ever came back to clear it all up," Lucy said.

While Nathan and the others began to set up the recording equipment, Avery went over and grabbed a fistful of the heavy red curtains obscuring the window. As she drew them aside, a cloud of dust billowed out from them. She let go, spluttering as she tried to wave the dust away from her eyes and nose.

"You alright over there?" Nathan asked.

She shot a thumbs up over her shoulder. "G-great," she wheezed, dragging the rest of the curtains aside to let in a thin stream of afternoon light. The clouds had descended thick and fast, covering most of the sky, and the room was still just as gloomy as before.

A draught was coming in from somewhere too, and Avery backed away from the window rubbing her arms. "I take it there's no central heating," she said. "Do you think there's any fuel for that fire?" She nodded towards the hearth, where the grate bled nothing but dry ash.

"Huh, good point. Does the place have an outhouse? Storeroom?" Randall said. "There might be some wood left around. As long as it hasn't been exposed to damp, it should still light."

"I'll go take a look," Avery suggested. She wanted to see more of the house anyway.

"I'll come with you," Caroline added. There was an uncertain edge to her expression, and Avery was curious to hear what the psychic was feeling about the house so far.

The two women left the sitting room in silence. Avery checked the cupboard beneath the stairs first, which harboured nothing but some old, mildewed furniture, and then the utility room, but there was no firewood. There was a door in the kitchen that led into the field at the rear of the property, so their last bet was if the house had some kind of storage shed.

The door was on a latch that could only be opened from the inside, but it was rusty from disuse and took several attempts to wriggle it free.

"Is everything okay, Caroline?" Avery asked as she finally unlatched the door, pausing with her hand resting against it.

"Yeah, everything's fine. Just tired from the journey."

"You seemed a little worried back there. Was there something about the room?"

She said nothing for a moment, then nodded, her eyes turning a cloudy shade of blue-grey. "There was… something *off* about it. I can't say what though. I just felt a little suffocated in there."

Avery chewed her lip. Caroline's predictions were never usually too far off the mark. If she felt uncomfortable in there, it was for a good reason.

"But I'm sure it's nothing," she added quickly. "I don't like saying anything unless I'm certain of what I'm feeling. I didn't spend long enough in there to really get a feel for the place."

Avery said nothing as she pushed open the door, a gust of wind immediately blowing through. The air had turned cold since that morning. There was a sharp chill now, and the wind had picked up, dragging her hair out behind her.

Beside the main property was a small outhouse made of reddish-brown brick. There was a single window, but most of it was obscured by thick cobwebs, and something inside was partially blocking it.

"Looks like some kind of work shed," Caroline said as the two of them approached it.

"I'm not sure if we'll find any wood inside, but it's worth a look."

"Let's hope it isn't locked," Avery added.

Caroline hummed in agreement, wrapping her arms around her waist as the wind picked up, scattering dry leaves across their path.

When they reached the shed, Avery hesitated before touching it. The door frame was swathed with cobwebs, and she could see little black husks of insects tucked away in the corners. But Caroline was shivering behind her, so she braved it and twisted the handle.

The door opened with a shudder, and a spider the size of her fingernail scuttled out from its web, causing Avery to flinch back. Caroline chuckled behind her. "Want me to go first?"

Avery grimaced at her childish display in front of the older woman, but nodded anyway, stepping aside to let Caroline pass.

The psychic went first, squinting as her eyes adjusted to the darkness inside, and Avery followed, careful not to brush her arms against the doorframe.

Inside the air smelt musty and damp, and when she glanced up, Avery could see a stain forming in the roof where water had been coming in. "If there is any wood in here, I'm not sure it'll be dry," she said, blowing out a sigh.

"Maybe not," Caroline said hopefully. "Look, under the workbench."

Avery followed her gaze to a small log store under the bench, tucked away in the shadows between a toolbox and an old-fashioned lawn mower.

"There might not be much inside, but I reckon it'll be better than freezing to death."

With the help of Avery, Caroline managed to drag the box out, pushing the lid onto the ground. A meagre stash of firewood was tucked inside, flaky but still dry. "This'll do," she said, picking up an armful of wood.

As Avery moved to grab the rest, something caught her attention and she whipped around.

For just a moment, it looked like someone had been peering through the window. It was only a glance in her periphery, but she was sure she had seen someone stood there.

Without a word, she left Caroline and darted back outside, turning wildly to see if anyone else was out there with them. But the field stretched on for miles, the long grass blowing in the wind, and there was nobody else around.

"Avery! You okay?" Caroline asked as she ran out after her a moment later.

"I... I thought I saw something," she said, turning to look at the window from the outside. Maybe she'd imagined it, or it had just been the wind, but she couldn't get the image out of her head that something had been there. "Never mind. It must have been nothing."

"You sure?" Caroline asked, glancing around them as the breeze stirred the grasses around their feet, bending the treetops in the distance.

"I'm sure. Come on, let's get back to the others."

Please remember to leave a review after reading.

Follow Eve S. Evans on instagram:

@eves.evansauthor

or

@foreverhauntedpodcast

Check out our Bone-Chilling Tales to keep you awake segment on youtube for more creepy, narriated and animated haunted stories by Eve S Evans.

Let me know on Instagram that you wrote a review and I'll send you a free copy of one of my other books!

Check out Eve on a weekly basis on one of her many podcasting ventures. Forever Haunted, The Ghosts That Haunt Me with Eve Evans, Bone Chilling Tales To Keep You Awake or A Truly Haunted Podcast. (On all podcasting networks.)

If you love to review books and would like a chance to snatch up one of Eve's ARCs before publication, follow her facebook page:

Eve S. Evans Author

For exclusive deals, ARCs, and giveaways!

FROM THE AUTHOR

After residing in two haunted houses in her lifetime, Eve Evans is enthralled with the world of paranormal. She writes ghost stories based on true events as well as fictional paranormal/horror novellas.

Eve is currently co-writing numerous books with author R Harrell and even delving into some fictional urban horror stories.

Check out her podcast for some audio ghost stories. Forever Haunted, A Truly Haunted Podcast, Bone-Chilling Tales To Keep You Awake Podcast And The Ghosts That Haunt Me.

Eve also runs the video channel Bone-Chilling Tales.

OTHER BOOKS YOU MAY

ENJOY

RECCOMENDED

BY EVE

FAKE NORA:
BY: KELLY MARTIN

The sign over the covered antique mirror said DO NOT TOUCH. Twelve-year-old Nora wished she had listened.

Mirrors reflect what is in front of them, but what happens behind the glass-to the reflections themselves? Nora finds out when her own reflection, aka Fake Nora, changes places with her one night. Nora is shoved in a place that looks exactly like her house with no echoes, dull lights, and muted sounds. It isn't her home at all, simply a shell of a place she loves.

Fake Nora is living her best life in Nora's house, feeding on the fear of her little brother while no one else at the house knows anything is wrong.

Inside "reflectionland," Nora meets thirteen-year-old Jesse, who has been stuck in his mirror since the forties, and he warns her that they aren't alone in the house. There are others sneaking around, known as the bad ones-spirits of people who gave up after vanishing in the mirror.

Refusing to stay a reflection forever, Nora conjures a plan to escape, but Fake Nora isn't about to give up her life in Nora's home. And Jesse? He could become a bad one forever.

★ ★ ★ ★ ★ "As if urban legends haven't given us enough reasons to be terrified of mirrors, Martin's FAKE NORA is sure to leave us clamoring to cover them all." - Lynn Shaw

★ ★ ★ ★ ★ "The novel is equivalent to a roller coaster ride, exhilarating, scary and ready to see how it ends!" – L Mallow

Made in the USA
Monee, IL
24 April 2022

95354558R00090